Robert Munsch

PLAYHOUSE

Illustrated by Michael Martchenko

Cartwheel
·B·O·O·K·S·®

SCHOLASTIC INC.

New York   Toronto   London   Auckland   Sydney
Mexico City   New Delhi   Hong Kong   Buenos Aires

The illustrations in this book were painted in watercolor on Arches paper.
The type is set in 18 point Frutiger.

Text copyright © 2002 by Bob Munsch Enterprises, Ltd.
Illustrations copyright © 2002 by Michael Martchenko.
All rights reserved. Published by Scholastic Inc.
ISBN 0-439-18772-9

Published simultaneously in Canada by Scholastic Canada Ltd.

Library of Congress Cataloging-in-Publication Data
Munsch, Robert N., 1945-
   Playhouse / by Robert Munsch ; illustrated by Michael Martchenko.
     p. cm.
   "Cartwheel books."
   Summary: Rene asks her father and mother to build her a playhouse, a play barn, a
play cow, and more, until finally her parents decide that they'd like to have a play Rene.
   ISBN 0-439-18772-9 (POB)
   [1. Greed--Fiction.] I. Martchenko, Michael, ill. II. Title.

PZ7.M927 Pl 2002
[E]--dc21

                                                          2001049316

      10 9 8 7 6 5 4 3 2 1   02 03 04 05 06 07
                  Printed in Canada
                First printing, April 2002

To Rene Jakubowski and her family,
Endeavour, Saskatchewan
— R.M.

One day, Rene went to her father and said, "Pleeeeeease make me a playhouse! Our farm is way out in the middle of the woods, and I have nobody to play with except my little brothers. I need a playhouse."

"Good idea," said Rene's father, and he made her a wonderful playhouse. It had real windows and a slide and a ladder and an upstairs and a downstairs. It was almost like a real house — but not quite.

The next day, Rene moved lots of stuff
from her room into the new playhouse,
and it was even more like a real house.
Then she drew fish all over the walls of
the playhouse, just like the ones on the
wall of her real bedroom.

Rene was happy for a whole week.
Then she went to her mother and said,
"Is this a city playhouse or a farm playhouse?"
"Well, Rene," said her mother, "we live on
a farm, so this must be a farm playhouse."

"Good," said Rene. "If it's a farm playhouse, it needs a play barn."

"A play what?" said her mother.

"A play barn," said Rene.

"I never heard of a play barn," said Rene's mother, but she was such a nice mother that she built Rene a play barn. It took her two weeks.

Rene moved some hay and some chickens from the real barn into her play barn, and it was almost like a real barn — but not quite.

Then Rene went to her father and said, "I need a play cow."

"A play what?" said her father.

"A play cow," said Rene. "A farm playhouse needs a play barn, needs a play cow."

"I can't build a play cow," said Rene's father, "and the play barn is not big enough for a real cow."

"No problem," said Rene. "How about you give me a goat and paint it so it looks like a cow, and then I will have a play cow."

So Rene's father got her a goat and painted it so it looked like a cow. Rene put her play cow, which was really a goat, in the play barn, and she felt like she had a farm of her own — but not quite.

Then Rene went to her father and said, "My play farm is out in the middle of the woods just like our real farm, so it needs the tractor and the bulldozer and the tree snipper and the log chopper. Why don't you just park them by my playhouse, and then you will not have to make me anything new?"

So her father parked the tractor and the bulldozer and the tree snipper and the log chopper beside the playhouse, and Rene played quite nicely for a whole month.

Then Rene went to her mother and said, "A farm playhouse needs a play barn, needs a play cow, needs a play tractor, needs a play mommy and a play daddy."

"A play who and a play what?" said her mother.

"A play mommy and a play daddy," said Rene.

"No," said Rene's mother. "You already have a real mommy and a real daddy. You don't need a play mommy and a play daddy."

"The real ones are too bossy," said Rene.

"Ha!" said her mother. "I am not going to make you a play mommy and a play daddy."

So Rene cut out a cardboard play mommy and a cardboard play daddy and stuck them on the side of her playhouse, and while she was at it, she made two play brothers.

When Rene came in for dinner, there was a scarecrow sitting in her chair.

"What's that?" said Rene.

"That," said her mother, "is my Play Rene. She is always nice and never bossy. You can eat play food out in the playhouse with your play mommy and your play daddy."

Rene said, "Play Rene and I are going to go outside."

Then the real Rene took Play Rene and fed it to the play cow, which was really a goat. The goat ate all the clothes and all the straw, and soon Play Rene was completely gone.

Then Rene walked into the kitchen and gave her mother a kiss.

"Was that a real kiss or a play kiss?" said Rene's mother.

"That," said Rene, "was a real kiss, from a real bossy daughter for a real bossy mommy. Now can I have a real dinner with my real family?"

"No problem," said her mother. "I like real bossy kids better than play kids anyway."

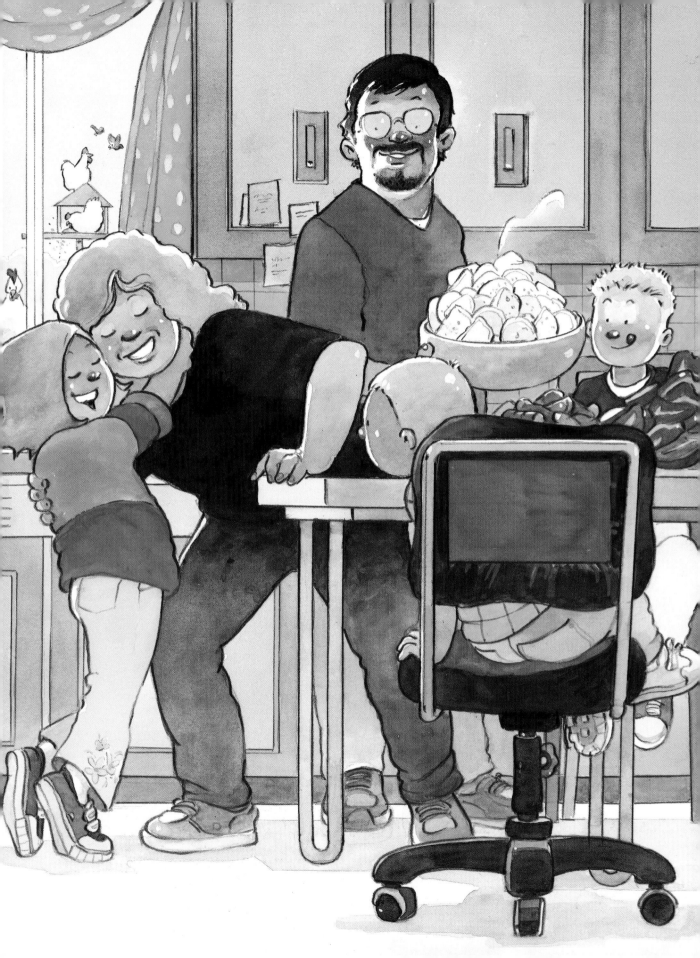

And everyone had a
real wonderful dinner.